A Parents Magazine
Read Aloud Original

MILK AND COOKIES

* A *
FRANK ASCH
Bear Story

Parents Magazine Press   *   New York

Library of Congress Cataloging in Publication Data
Asch, Frank. Milk and cookies. (A Frank Asch Bear Story)
SUMMARY: While spending the night at Grandfather's
house, Baby Bear dreams of feeding milk and cookies
to a dragon.
[1. Bears—Fiction. 2. Dreams—Fiction.]
I. Title. II. Series: Asch, Frank. Bear story.
PZ7.A778Mi 1982   [E]   82-7962
ISBN 0-8193-1087-5   AACR2
ISBN 0-8193-1088-3 (lib. bdg.)

To my uncles,
who love their wood stoves.

One winter day, the Bear family
went to visit Grandma and Grandpa.

When it got to be late,
too late to go home . . .

Grandma made up the couch
for them in the living room.

"Good night," said Grandma
and Grandpa.
"Good night," said Mama and Papa.
"Good night," said Baby Bear.

And they all went to sleep.

In the middle of the night,
Baby Bear heard a noise
and woke up.
Then he saw a strange red light
coming from under the cellar door.

He climbed out of bed,
and tiptoed to the door
to see what it was.

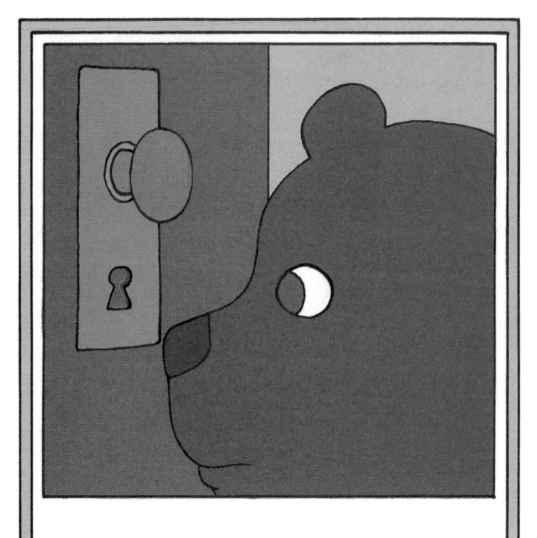

He didn't want to make any noise,
so he just peeked through the keyhole.

What he saw looked like
a giant dragon with flames
shooting from its mouth.
Grandpa was there feeding it.

When the dragon shut its mouth,
Grandpa came upstairs.
"Is there anything wrong?"
asked Grandpa.
"No, I'm OK," said Baby Bear.

"Would you like some
milk and cookies?" asked Grandpa.
"No, thank you," said Baby Bear.
And he went back to bed.

That night Baby Bear dreamed
that the cellar door opened,

and the dragon . . .

came upstairs!

"I'm hungry," said the dragon.

Baby Bear ran into the kitchen,

and opened the refrigerator.

He poured the dragon a glass of milk,

and opened a box of cookies.

"Thank you," said the dragon.
"I like milk and cookies."

And he ate everything all up.

He didn't save any milk
or even one cookie
for Baby Bear.

Just then Baby Bear
woke up crying.

Mama and Papa Bear woke up too.

Baby Bear told them his dream.

"Whatever gave you the idea that there was a dragon in the cellar?" asked Mama Bear.
"I saw it!" said Baby Bear.

"If I come downstairs with you,"
asked Papa Bear,
"will you show me the dragon?"
"OK," said Baby Bear.
And they went downstairs.

In the corner where Baby Bear
thought he had seen a dragon,

there was a wood stove.

Papa Bear opened the door.

Inside, the flames glowed brightly.

"There, you see," said Papa Bear.
"There is no dragon in the cellar,
just an old wood stove."

When they went back upstairs,
Grandma and Grandpa were up.
"Is everything all right?"
asked Grandma.
"It is now," said Papa Bear.

"Good!" said Grandpa.

"Let's all have some . . .

milk and cookies!"

About the Author/Artist

FRANK ASCH published his first children's book in 1968 and since then has created many award-winning picture books. For Parents Magazine Press, he has written and illustrated four much-loved Bear Stories: *Milk and Cookies, Sandcake, Popcorn,* and *Bread and Honey.*

As an artist, Mr. Asch explores color and shape each in its simplest possible form. His goal is to enable a child to absorb an entire illustration quickly and easily. When a child sees an illustration clearly, he or she can hear the full meaning of the words at the same time. Pictures and story have a simultaneous impact.

Frank Asch and his family live in Middletown Springs, Vermont, where Mr. Asch often conducts story hour at the local library.